BLOOD 4 BLOOD

Leu Ce Pher

authorHOUSE®

AuthorHouse™
1663 Liberty Drive
Bloomington, IN 47403
www.authorhouse.com
Phone: 1-800-839-8640

First published by AuthorHouse 7/22/2009

ISBN: 978-1-4389-9345-4 (sc)

Library of Congress Control Number: 2009906925

Printed in the United States of America
Bloomington, Indiana
This book is printed on acid-free paper.

Several cases of police brutality and wrongful
deaths flash after one another.

On March 3, 1991, Rodney Glen King, an African-American male
was a victim of a vicious assault by four LAPD officers.

The four officers were later tried in a state court for
the beating but were acquitted. The announcement of the
acquittals has sparked riots all over Los Angeles.

Four New York policemen shot and killed 23 year-old Guinean
immigrant Amadou Diallo on February 4, 1999 in front of his
home. The four officers were cleared of criminal wrongdoing
in the West African immigrants' death.

On November 25, 2006, NYPD officers opened fire on one Latino
and two African-American men a total of fifty times and killed
African-American male Sean Bell, severely wounding his
two friends. Three of the five detectives involved in the
shooting went to trial on charges ranging from manslaughter
to reckless endangerment, and were found not guilty.

Glimpses of another case are shown in steps.

It is pouring rain outside and the sirens are loud.

OFFICER 1: (ON THE WALKIE TALKIE)

We have visual of possible suspect.

DISPATCHER:

Roger that.

OFFICER 2:

Stop right there!
Don't move!

TERRENCE PRICE:

What's going on?

OFFICER 3:

Don't move you son of a bitch.

TERRENCE PRICE:

Hey I didn't do anything wrong, look my
brother is a special agent for one of you
big dogs, let me call him.

OFFICER 3:

I said don't move!

Terrence Price reaches for his cell phone,
he starts to pull it out.

OFFICER 2:

He's got a gun!

OFFICER 1:

Fire!

Each officer empty's a full magazine into
Terrence Price.

OFFICER 1: (ON THE WALKIE TALKIE)

Suspect is down,
I repeat suspect is down.

DISPATCHER:

Roger that.

FADE TO INSIDE A COURTROOM WHERE EACH OFFI-
CER IS TELLING THEIR STORY OF WHAT HAPPENED
THAT NIGHT. WE GLIMPSE AT DIFFERENT PARTS
OF THEIR STORIES IN SEQUENCE.

LAWYER:

What happened that night?

OFFICER 1:

We saw a person fitting the description of our suspect.

OFFICER 2:

We had ordered him to stop.

OFFICER 3:

He started pulling something from his pocket, we were afraid for our lives.

LAWYER:

So what did you do next?

OFFICER 1:

We opened fire.

OFFICER 2:

We opened fire.

OFFICER 3:

We opened fire.

JURY FOREPERSON:

In the case against officers Martin Monroe, Jack Seiver, and Anthony Beans, on the charges of manslaughter and murder in the 1st degree, we find in favor of the defendants' not guilty.

CROWD: (SCREAMING AND YELLING)

No, that's not right.

MOTHER PRICE:

They murdered my baby. Those monsters murdered my baby.Kenneth Price is holding his mother, trying to calm her down.

TV REPORTER:

In the case against the three officer's involving the death of 19 year-old African-American male Terrence Price, the officer's were found not guilty.

                                    FADE TO BLACK.
A YEAR LATER.

Scenes of New York precincts are being shown, each borough, different precincts. We see people getting on top of roofs, setting up for something. Glimpse by glimpse, we see rocket launchers coming out of bags; the groups take aim at the precincts and fire. People are panicking and going crazy, wondering what's going on.

Were inside the office of the Commissioner.

COMMISSIONER STYLES: (YELLING ON THE PHONE)

Listen to me very carefully, I need to know what precinct are still standing do you hear me. Send medics to the ones that are gone to see if anyone is still alive. Get the fire departments on sight for both rescue and recover. I need to know what precincts are still standing. Get on it. **(He hangs up the phone)**

OFFICER: (BARGING THROUGH THE DOOR)

Sir?!

COMMISSIONER STYLES:

What?!

OFFICER:

The Mayor is on the phone.

COMMISSIONER STYLES:

Yes Mr. Mayor?

MAYOR:

Styles what the fuck is happening to my
city?
Is it terrorist attacks?

COMMISSIONER STYLES:

I don't know sir, but rest a sure that I am
doing everything to find out.

MAYOR:

Well you had better, I want some fucking
answers. The damn media is outside
demanding answers, and I have nothing to
tell them.

COMMISSIONER STYLES:

Mr. Mayor, I am trying my best to figure out
what the hell is going on, as soon as I
know anything you will be the first to know.

MAYOR:

I had better.

(He hangs up the phone)

COMMISSIONER STYLES:

Jesus fucking Christ, what's happened to my
city?

COMMISSIONER STYLES:

What?!

KENNETH PRICE:

Commissioner Styles, how are you doing
today?

COMMISSIONER STYLES:

Who the fuck is this?

KENNETH PRICE:

We will get to that soon enough, but first I would like for you to meet me at the 2nd precinct.

COMMISSIONER STYLES:

And why the hell would I want to do that?

KENNETH PRICE:

Because if you don't commissioner, I will take out another precinct.

COMMISSIONER STYLES:

Wait! What?! Who is this?!

KENNETH PRICE:

You have 20 minutes commissioner, 20 minutes and not a minute more.

(He hangs up the phone)

COMMISSIONER STYLES:

Wait! Hello! Hello! Shit!

(He storms off)

FADE TO THE COMMISSIONER ENTERING THE 2ND PRECINCT.

COMMISSIONER STYLES: (LOOKING AROUND)

Alright, where are you, you son of a bitch?

CAPTAIN WILLIAMS:

Commissioner?! Why are you here?

COMMISSIONER STYLES:

I got a phone call saying I better be here in 20 minutes or another precinct was going to be taken out.

CAPTAIN WILLIAMS:

What, the asshole called you?!

COMMISSIONER STYLES:

Yea, so where is he?! The phone rings.

CAPTAIN WILLIAMS:

Hello!

KENNETH PRICE:

Is the Commissioner there?

CAPTAIN WILLIAMS:

Who is this?

KENNETH PRICE:

I just wish to know if the commissioner is there

CAPTAIN WILLIAMS?

Captain Williams: (Looking at the Commissioner)
Yea he's here.

KENNETH PRICE:

Good, if you would be so kind to put me on speaker please.

CAPTAIN WILLIAMS:

Yea, hold on.

(Pushes the speaker button)

COMMISSIONER STYLES:

Everyone quiet, I said quiet damn it!

KENNETH PRICE:

Hello everyone. How are you all doing today?

COMMISSIONER STYLES:

Who are you and what do you want?

KENNETH PRICE:

I see you wish to dispense with the pleasantries'. Alright then, I'm okay with that. I am former ATF Special Agent Kenneth Price.

CAPTAIN WILLIAMS:

Price?

KENNETH PRICE:

That's right Captain Williams, Price. My brother was Terrence Price; he would have been 20 years-old this year, if he wasn't murdered last year, this date.

COMMISSIONER STYLES:

20 minutes.

KENNETH PRICE:

That is right Commissioner, 20.

CAPTAIN WILLIAMS:

What do you want?

KENNETH PRICE:

What I want is very simple. Your man Martin Monroe, Jack Seiver, and Anthony Beans, murdered my brother; they murdered a badges family member. Deliver them to the same street that is soaked with my brother's blood. I do not want them dead, just delivered. I know that Jack Seiver works desk there, deliver him to me.

COMMISSIONER STYLES:

And if we don't?

KENNETH PRICE:

Than every hour I will take out another
precinct until I have the three of them.
Even if one is delivered to me, I will
spare a precinct that hour. And if run
out of precincts, I will find other targets
until I get exactly what I want.

CAPTAIN WILLIAMS:

What haven't you taken out this precinct?
This is where they came from.

KENNETH PRICE:

I have my reason's Captain Williams, I have
my reason's. Your first hour starts now.

(He hangs up the phone)

COMMISSIONER STYLES:

Did anyone get a trace?

OFFICER:

No sir, the signal was being re-routed all
over, he's good.

COMMISSIONER STYLES:

No shit he's good, get me ATF on the phone,
now!!

Forward to a secretary walking extremely
fast into the director of ATF's office.

SECRETARY:

Sir, we have a problem in New York.
He looks at her with a frightened look on
his face.

FADE TO A BEDROOM WHERE SPECIAL AGENT

Tanya Snow is giving head to Special Agent Joseph Gears.
Her head is moving up and down, her hand stroking his dick.
She's slurping; he's grabbing her head and moaning. He
climax's in her mouth, she swallows and wipes her mouth, they
both laugh. She starts to kiss his stomach, and move up his
body, he grabs her by the hair and kisses her.

AGENT SNOW:

My turn.

She lays flat on her back and spreads her legs in 90 degree
angels. Agent Gears starts to go down on her, she starts to
moan and groan. A cell phone rings.

AGENT SNOW:

It's yours.

AGENT GEARS:

Who is it?

AGENT SNOW:

It's the director.

AGENT GEARS:

He wouldn't be calling unless it was
important.
Pass it here, hey boss, what's up?

DIRECTOR KELPS:

Hey Gears, look I know it's your time off
and all, but we have a situation in New
York.

AGENT GEARS:

No, no, what's the situation?

DIRECTOR KELPS:

Price Gears,
Price is our situation.

Zooming in on Agent Gears' face, we fade to where there all in the ATF kitchen and Price is trashing the place after hearing news of his brother. Agent Gears is trying to calm him down.

KENNETH PRICE: (CRYING AND BREAKING THINGS)

They murdered my brother Joseph, those local pigs murdered my brother.

AGENT GEARS: (TRYING TO HOLD HIM DOWN)

I know Price, I know.
I'm sorry, I'm so sorry.

KENNETH PRICE:

They'll pay for this,
I'll get them all for this.

Agent Gears is still holding him down,
Price is crying and kicking.

Agent Snow is in the corner sitting and
crying for Price, while Director Kelps is
standing by the entrance of the Kitchen,
looking over them all.

      FADE BACK TO A HELICOPTER TAKING OFF, HEAD-
          ING TOWARDS NEW YORK.

Agent Gears is checking his watch.

AGENT SNOW:

Are you okay?!

AGENT GEARS:

I just can't believe Price is behind all
this!

AGENT SNOW:

You and I both know why he's doing this!

AGENT GEARS:

That doesn't make it right Snow,
that doesn't make it right!

AGENT SNOW:

I'm not saying that Gears! I'm not saying
that at all! But you and I both saw how
messed up he was after his brother's death,
he wasn't the same again!

AGENT GEARS:

Yea, I know, I know.

                                    FADE BACK TO THE PRECINCT.

The television is on.

TV REPORTER:

Excuse me Mr. Mayor, what can you tell us
about these attacks on the precincts?

MAYOR:

At this time I can't tell you anything,
this is an ongoing investigation and we are
doing everything and anything to find out
who is responsible for what is going on
here.

TV REPORTER:

Are these terrorist attacks?

MAYOR:

I don't know anything for sure, when I know
something, you'll know something. Excuse
me.

TV REPORTERS:

Mr. Mayor, Mr. Mayor!!!!

Back inside the precinct.

OFFICER:

Sir, two ATF agents will be here in 15.

COMMISSIONER STYLES:

Leys hope they could give us some insight into this Price guy. How much time we have before the next attack?

OFFICER:

About 20 minutes, sir.

COMMISSIONER STYLES:

Shit!

CAPTAIN WILLIAMS:

You really think he'll take out another precinct?

COMMISSIONER STYLES:

No doubt in my mind he will.

They both stare at a clock count down.

FADE TO A HELICOPTER LANDING.

AGENT SNOW:

How much time do we have?!

AGENT GEARS:

Not much, get in!

They get into a car and take off.

We arrive in front of the 2nd precinct.
They get out of the car.

AGENT GEARS: (CHECKING HIS WATCH)

Times up.

WE FADE TO PRICE CHECKING RUBBING HIS CHIN,
HAVING A FLASHBACK OF HIS OWN.

Were at Kenneth Price's graduation from ATF school, he's with
his mother and a younger Terrence Price.

MOTHER PRICE:

I'm so proud of you son.

KENNETH PRICE:

Thank you mom.

TERRENCE PRICE:

My brother the big ATF agent. Sounds like
one of those rich white boy organizations.
What does it stand for again?

KENNETH PRICE:

Alcohol, Tobacco, Firearms.

TERRENCE PRICE:

Yea, definitely one of theirs.

MOTHER PRICE:

Oh leave your brother alone, let me get a
picture of us all. Excuse me sir, can you
take a picture of me and my boys.

KENNETH PRICE:

Mother, that's my new boss, Director Kelps.

DIRECTOR KELPS:

Hahaha, its cool Agent Price, I would be
honored. You were top of your class; I got
lucky to get you. You must be very proud
ma'me?

MOTHER PRICE:

Oh, I am. Thank you.
Everyone say cheese.

KENNETH AND TERRENCE PRICE:

Oh mom.

MOTHER PRICE:

Just say it.

DIRECTOR KELPS:

Listen to your mother.
Everyone says cheese,

Director Kelps takes the picture.

KENNETH PRICE:

Thank you director.

DIRECTOR KELPS:

No problem Price, see you soon.
Good-bye, take care.

(He walks off)

MOTHER AND TERRENCE PRICE:

Bye!

TERRENCE PRICE:

So does this mean, I'm officially never,
ever going to get into trouble again?

KENNETH PRICE:

What it means is, I'm always going to
protect you, always.

Kenneth Price grabs Terrence head and pulls
him in.

He kisses him on the forehead.

KENNETH PRICE:

I love you little brother.

TERRENCE PRICE:

I love you too big brother, and I am proud
of you.

KENNETH PRICE:

Thank you.

They hug.

Mother Price takes a picture of them.

KENNETH AND TERRENCE PRICE:

Mommm!

MOTHER PRICE:

Oh hush, let me get in on this hug.

They all hug and laugh.

                    FADE BACK TO KENNETH PRICE.

FOOT SOLDIER:

Price, still no murderers delivered to us.

KENNETH PRICE:

Send word to take out another precinct.

FOOT SOLDIER:

Roger that.

Back to the precinct, Agents Gears and Snow
enter the precinct, but not before hearing
another huge explosion.

AGENT SNOW:

He took out another one.

AGENT GEARS:

Damn it Price.

They move in to the precinct where they see everyone else.

AGENT GEARS:

Commissioner Styles?

COMMISSIONER STYLES:

Yea that's me!
Are you my agents?

AGENT GEARS:

Special Agent Joseph Gears and
Special Agent Tanya Snow.

AGENT SNOW:

Hi.

COMMISSIONER STYLES:

Yea, hi. This is Captain Williams.

CAPTAIN WILLIAMS:

Are you gonna help us catch this dirt bag.

The phone rings.

CAPTAIN WILLIAMS:

Hello. (Pause) Its him.

(Pushes the speaker button)

KENNETH PRICE:

Calling my bluff was not very wise.

AGENT GEARS:

I don't think they were calling your bluff
Price.

KENNETH PRICE:

Joseph, is that you?

AGENT GEARS:

Yea Price, it's me.

KENNETH PRICE:

Well, it's been awhile old friend.
How's everything been going?

AGENT GEARS:

Good, up till now.

KENNETH PRICE:

Hmmm, how's Tanya?

AGENT SNOW:

I'm here Ken.
And I'm doing just fine.

KENNETH PRICE:

Has he popped the question yet?

AGENT SNOW:

No, not yet.

KENNETH PRICE:

Joseph, you disappoint me, that's a good
woman right there, what are you waiting
for?

COMMISSIONER STYLES:

Hey look I don't mean to break up this
love fest over here, but my city has been
reduced to rubble, I've got dead cops
turning up left and right, and I want it to
stop, right now.

KENNETH PRICE:

I told you how to make this stop,
you have a hearing problem I suppose.

COMMISSIONER STYLES:

Listen here you son of a bitch, I will
fucking murder you, you hear me, I will
fucking murder you.

KENNETH PRICE:

Joseph shut him up right now,
you hear me, shut him up.

AGENT GEARS:

Shut up okay, just shut your fucking mouth!

KENNETH PRICE:

Take me off speaker Joseph.

AGENT GEARS:

Yea Price.

KENNETH PRICE:

You know what happened to my brother was
wrong, don't you?

AGENT GEARS:

What do you call this Price?

KENNETH PRICE:

LA called it riots, I call this justice.
Listen to me very carefully Gears, are you
listening?

AGENT GEARS:

Yea Price,
I'm listening.

KENNETH PRICE:

Jack Seiver, one of the men that murdered
my brother, he works desk there, have him
delivered to me, and you get to save a
precinct in the next hour.

AGENT GEARS: (LOOKING AT JACK SEIVER)

You know I can't and will not do that
Price.

KENNETH PRICE:

Then say good-bye to another precinct
Gears.

(Hangs up the phone)

AGENT GEARS:

Wait Price! Price!

(Slams the phone down)

> FADE TO THE WAREHOUSE PRICE IS OPERATING
> FROM.

The warehouse is filled with weapons, cameras, computers and
anything else that helps them operate.

FOOT SOLDIER:

What the word boss?

KENNETH PRICE:

Prepare to take out another
precinct in the next hour.

FOOT SOLDIER:

You heard him, get word out, another
precinct goes.

Back to the 2nd precinct.

AGENT SNOW:

What did he say?

AGENT GEARS:

Are you Jack Seiver, one of the officer's
involved in Terrence Price's shooting?

JACK SEIVER:

Yes Sir.

AGENT GEARS:

Get him to the back, we don't need him up
here.
We all know of a story that happened that
night.

CAPTAIN WILLIAMS:

Get him back there.
What do you mean a story?

AGENT GEARS:

I mean the story that your officers gave,
the only stories that will ever be heard.

CAPTAIN WILLIAMS:

Hey fuck you! Don't come into my house
talking this shit!
My men did their jobs, were all don't
apologizing for this!
It was an accident!

AGENT GEARS:

It's amazing how many accidents you
local police officers have.

CAPTAIN WILLIAMS:

Hey at least we don't have a rogue agent
killing countless cops and innocent
bystanders!

AGENT GEARS:

No, you just kill innocent bystanders one
at a time!

CAPTAIN WILLIAMS:

Fuck you!

AGENT GEARS:

Oh yea,
you wanna go!

A huge fight breaks out, fists are thrown. Everyone gets in
to break it up. Agent Snow fires three rounds into the air,
everyone stops and looks at her.

AGENT SNOW:

Look I understand we are dealing with a
threat that none of us ever expected to
deal with, especially from one of our own,
former or not. But we have this threat
nonetheless, and we are not going to deal
with it by turning on each other. We all
still have a badge and an oath to abide by,
so calm the fuck down!!

In the back room, officer Jack Seiver looks
outside and sees what's going on. He takes
his badge off and puts it on the table. He
then takes off his officer belt and places
that on the table as well. He secretly
takes off. Another officer
watches him take off.

AGENT SNOW:

Where are the other two involved in the
shooting of Terrence Price?

CAPTAIN WILLIAMS:

We have no idea, after what happened,
they all went elsewhere.

COMMISSIONER STYLES:

Why is he going about this, this way? Not
that I want this, why not just go after
those three personally?

AGENT GEARS:

Because the message wouldn't be heard
right. This way everyone has to listen,
they have to take notice. Three cops end
up dead, the message isn't loud enough
to make people hear, but countless cops
turning dead, everyone pays attention, they
have to.

AGENT SNOW:

They news doesn't know anything, right?

COMMISSIONER STYLES:

No, we've kept them in the dark.

AGENT SNOW:

Good, let's keep it that way.

COMMISSIONER STYLES:

How is it possible that he has all this man
power?

CAPTAIN WILLIAMS:

Huh, are you kidding, people hate us,
especially gang bangers and other supposed
victims. And if this is about what
happened to his brother……

AGENT GEARS: (CUTTING HIM OFF)

This is about his brother!

They share dirty looks.

AGENTS GEARS:

This is about his brother, his mother that
died from a heart attack days later. That
what all this comes down to.

CAPTAIN WILLIAMS:

Well I'll be the first to admit, he's going to have a lot of followers wanting to help him wipe us off the face off the earth.

COMMISSIONER STYLES:

What about the arsenal he has, how did he gain control of all the weaponry?

Agents Gears and Snow look at one another.

COMMISSIONER STYLES:

You two know don't you?

AGENT SNOW:

Sometime last year, we had this case, a shipment of weapons just disappeared of our manifest. We don't know why or how it happened?

COMMISSIONER STYLES:

We do now!
Wasn't their investigation?

AGENT GEARS:

Of course there was, but we couldn't find anything. We had our suspicions it was an inside job, but nothing leading us to anyone definitively.

CAPTAIN WILLIAMS:

And Price?

AGENT GEARS:

He quit the agency several months after the verdict came in of his brother's killers.

CAPTAIN WILLIAMS:

And that didn't raise suspicions for you?

AGENT SNOW:

There was no reason for us to suspect
him, he was our friend, and he was one of
ours. And besides all that he quit before
the weapons were stolen, he wasn't on the
inside anymore.

COMMISSIONER STYLES:

That doesn't mean he didn't know how to
work the system now does it?

AGENTS GEARS:

We all know how to work the system here,
don't we?

COMMISSIONER STYLES:

Hey listen here……

(His phone rings)

Shit, it's the Mayor. Excuse me.

CAPTAIN WILLIAMS:

We need to find him,
and put an end to this.

AGENT SNOW:

All we know for sure is that he's close to
where his brother died, he must have that
area watched like a hawk eye.

CAPTAIN WILLIAMS:

What type of weapons specifically does he
have?

WE FADE INTO PRICE'S AREA OF OPERATION,
WERE THESE WEAPONS ARE BEING SHOWN.

AGENT GEARS:

Huh, according to the manifest of the
shipment that we lost,saw gunners, small
firearms, rocket launchers, rifles, you name
it, he has, they are ready for anything.

FOOT SOLDIER:

Hey Price, we have Jack Seiver on camera.

KENNETH PRICE:

Where?

FOOT SOLDIER:

About a block away from where Terrence was
murdered.

KENNETH PRICE:

Get this up on the internet and broadcast
live, I want the whole world to see this.
Let's go!

Officer Jack Seiver is wondering through the streets, it has
been completely deserted and sealed off except for certain
areas for people to come and go.

OFFICER JACK SEIVER:

I'm here! You hear me, I came!
Now come and take me!

Kenneth Price shows up with his crew. They get out and half
surround him.

KENNETH PRICE:

Hello Officer Seiver,
I see you've come on your own.

OFFICER JACK SEIVER:

I don't want to be responsible for anymore
dead cops.

KENNETH PRICE:

No, of course not,
just responsible for my dead brother.

FOOT SOLDIER:

Were up Price.

Back at the precinct.

OFFICER:

We have something on the TV!

Everyone turns to view it.

CAPTAIN WILLIAMS:

Is that Seiver?

An officer is running back to check.

OFFICER:

Seiver is gone, left his badge and belt.

CAPTAIN WILLIAMS:

Fuck!

COMMISSIONER STYLES:

Get some people over there!

AGENT SNOW:

You can't!

COMMISSIONER STYLES:

What?! Why not?!

AGENT SNOW:

I've been mapping out the explosions,
he strategically took out precincts that
would pose a threat and you don't have the
man power to stop him. He's thought this
through.

Agent snow has a flashback of a similar time Price did something that was strategic. Were in a hotel room, Agent Gears enters and finds Agent Snow there.

AGENT SNOW:

Hey.

AGENT GEARS:

Hey, what are you doing here?

AGENT SNOW:

Kenneth told me to meet him here.

AGENT GEARS:

He told me to meet him here.

KENNETH PRICE:

I told you both too meet me here, to meet each other. You white folks aren't the smartest bunch in the world, sometimes you need a little push to get the ball rolling.

AGENT GEARS:

Price……

KENNETH PRICE:

Don't Price me Joseph, you care for her and you care for him. Whatever it is, you two need to work it out.

(He walks off and closes the door behind him)

AGENT SNOW:

He's a strategist that one.

AGENT GEARS:

Yea, he's always been.
So how do you want to work this out?

AGENT SNOW: (DROPPING HER GOWN)

I think we should get the sex out of the
way first, than talk.

AGENT GEARS:

I agree.

He grabs her and kisses her, she jumps on
him and wraps her legs around his waist.
He forces himself and her against the wall,
he holds her hand against the wall and
starts to go down on her.

                                    FADE BACK TO THE PRECINCT.

AGENT GEARS:

He made sure you didn't have enough man
power to stop this, you could get there,
but have no means of defending yourself if
more of his people came out.

CAPTAIN WILLIAMS:

Well get the national guard!

COMMISSIONER STYLES:

There busy cleaning up other areas,
we can't ask them to stop for one guy!

CAPTAIN WILLIAMS:

That's one of my own commissioner!

COMMISSIONER STYLES:

I know Williams, but what do you want me to
do?

AGENT GEARS:

Everyone stop, look you told me he said he
didn't want them dead right?

COMMISSIONER STYLES:

Yea, that's what he said.

AGENT GEARS:

Then we'll wait and see what happens next.

Back to Price and Seiver.

KENNETH PRICE:

You took my brother from me,
and this is what I have resolved myself to
become.

OFFICER JACK SEIVER:

I am so sorry for your brother,
I really am, it was a mistake.

KENNETH PRICE: (TOSSING HIM SOMETHING)

Read this.

OFFICER JACK SEIVER:

What is it?

KENNETH PRICE:

Read it.

OFFICER JACK SEIVER:

Why?

KENNETH PRICE:

I said read it!

OFFICER JACK SEIVER: (CRYING)

Last year myself and two other officers took the life of an unarmed man. We murdered him, by the abuse of the badge and the legal system we got away with murder. We should have been found guilty, that should have been the verdict.
The penalty for the murder of Terrence Price is……

KENNETH PRICE:

Say it.

OFFICER JACK SEIVER: (BEGGING)

Please don't.

KENNETH PRICE:

Say it now!

OFFICER JACK SEIVER:

The penalty for the murder of Terrence Price is death.

Kenneth Price and two other foot soldiers pull out 9mm Berettas, resembling the ones used to kill Terrence.

Each man empties a full magazine into Officer Jack Seiver.

KENNETH PRICE:

Let's move out.

Back at the precinct.

AGENT SNOW:

I can't believe he did that.

The phone rings.

CAPTAIN WILLIAMS:

You son of a bitch, I swear to god I am
going to gut you!

KENNETH PRICE:

You can't gut me Captain,
I'm no longer a pig.

(Laughing follows)

CAPTAIN WILLIAMS:

You think this is funny, I'm going to
murder you, I give you my word, you'll die
for this, all of it.

AGENT GEARS:

Give me the phone, give me the phone!
Price, what the fuck, I was informed you
didn't want them dead.

KENNETH PRICE:

I didn't want them delivered to me dead
Joseph, I'm sorry if I wasn't more clear.

AGENT GEARS:

Damn it Price, you want these men delivered
to you so you could just murder them in
cold blood!

KENNETH PRICE:

I want blood for blood Joseph! Blood for
blood.
I want to spill the blood of these pigs the
same way they spilled my brother's blood.
I want their blood spilled in the same fear
and terror as they spilled Terrence's on
the same street that is soaked with his
blood.

AGENT GEARS:

We won't give you them, not the other two,
not after what we just saw.

KENNETH PRICE:

I am fully aware what you will and will not
do, but what about the general public, what
will they do?

AGENT GEARS:

What are you talking about Price?

KENNETH PRICE:

You'll see soon enough Joseph, you'll see
soon enough.

(He hangs up the phone)

Agent Gears hangs up the phone.

AGENT SNOW:

What now Gears?

AGENT GEARS:

He says well know soon enough.

COMMISSIONER STYLES:

What the hell does that mean?

FADE TO PRICE GIVING ORDERS.

KENNETH PRICE:

Alright, I want everything up ASAP,
we are going to plan B.

Everyone is running around getting whatever
they need done.

FOOT SOLDIER:

One down boss.

KENNETH PRICE:

Two to go,
two to go.

FADE BACK TO THE PRECINCT WITH SOMETIME BE-
ING PASSED.

AGENT SNOW:

Look at that?

AGENT GEARS:

What?

AGENT SNOW:

The TV, turn it up!

KENNETH PRICE:

Hello ladies and gentlemen of the general
public. I am Kenneth Price, if you
remember my brother was Terrence Price, he
was murdered last year. I am responsible
for the chaos that has gone down today, I
had informed the 2nd precinct on the attacks
and why it was happening; but it seems
they have decided to keep you all in the
dark. They have decided you didn't have
the right to know why your city has become
a blood bath, so I will inform you. Every
hour I will take out another precinct until
this man Martin Monroe and this man Anthony
Beans are delivered to me on the streets
where they murdered my brother. I will
be happy with one at a time, but it won't
stop definitively until I eventually have
them both. If you don't know, just ask
them, I'm sure they would remember. As
I told the authorities, if I run out of
precincts, I will be so incline to other
targets. This decision to include you
is my decision; I felt it was best that
you civilians get to decide for yourself
your own fates. To keep up with the whole
premise of things, I will now take out
another precinct, do it now. Deliver those
men to me alive, clocks ticking.

COMMISSIONER STYLES:

Is he out of his fucking mind?
How do you people hire someone like that?

AGENT GEARS:

I don't think you wanna go down that rabbit
hole again?

AGENT SNOW:

Look we don't have time to measure dick
sizes, Captain get all available man and
find those two.

CAPTAIN WILLIAMS:

I'm on it.

AGENT SNOW:

Gears, he has completely lost it.

AGENT GEARS:

Has he?

                    FADE TO THE WAREHOUSE.

FOOT SOLDIER:

Are you sure this is going to work
boss,that they'll bring them to us?

KENNETH PRICE:

It's human nature to want to survive,
protect your own. These people will bring
Monroe and Beans to us, I'm sure of it.

            FADE TO A LOCAL BAR, MARTIN MONROE HAS HIS
            SHARE OF PROBLEMS WITH THE BARTENDER AND
                            SOME USUALS.

MARTIN MONROE:

Hey look guys; I know what you're thinking,
but take it easy.

BARTENDER PHIL:

Hey Martin, just listen to what we have to say.

MARTIN MONROE:

I'm walking out of here Phil, okay, that's it.

Some men get up and lock the door, and then a stand post.

MARTIN MONROE:

Tell them to move Phil, right now!

BARTENDER PHIL:

Martin, you heard this guy, he just wants you and Beans, than all this can stop. Don't you want that?

MARTIN MONROE:

Yea, so we could end up like Jack. Sorry that's not happening to me. No way!

Some of the men move in closer, martin draws his weapon.

MARTIN MONROE:

Get back, you hear me get back right now, unlock the fucking door!

BARTENDER PHIL: (REACHING FOR SOMETHING)

Look Martin, calm down okay.

(His hand rises)

Martin fires two shots in his chest. The bartender goes down. The other men make an attempt to catch him while he's briefly distracted; he shoots and kills them as well.

He runs out of the bar.

FADE TO ANTHONY BEANS GETTING HIS FAMILY
OUT OF THE AREA AS SOON AS HE CAN.

MARY BEANS:

Baby, why are we doing this, these people
won't hurt us. They're our friends.

ANTHONY BEANS:

They'll do anything to protect themselves,
even deliver me to that monster.

CHILD:

Daddy look!

ANTHONY BEANS:

Tom? Billy?

TOM:

Let's go Anthony.

ANTHONY BEANS:

Let's go where?

BILLY:

Please Anthony; he just wants you and that
other guy, then he swears it will all stop.

ANTHONY BEANS:

Listen here assholes, we all saw what he
did to that cop Jack Seiver, the other
cop that was involved with his brother's
murder, shooting, with his brother's
shooting.

BILLY:

Now we know what happened that night.

ANTHONY BEANS:

Fuck you, it was a clean shoot. You really
think he'll stop after he gets me?

TOM:

Yea we do Tony.

BILLY:

Let's go Anthony!

ANTHONY BEANS:

I'm not going anywhere with you two.
Now get the fuck out of my way.

Anthony goes to reach for his weapon, but a
couple of guys grab him from behind.

MARY BEANS:

Anthony!!!!!!

CHILD:

Daddy!!!!!!

MARY BEANS:

Jesus Christ Tom, were your friends.

TOM:

Sorry Mary, my son's precinct hasn't been
hit yet, I gotta do this.

MARY BEANS:

Anthony!

ANTHONY BEANS:

Get the fuck out of here Mary, drive off!

MARY BEANS:

I can't just leave you!

CHILD:

Daddy!!

ANTHONY BEANS:

I love you both very much, now go!

Mary Beans hops into the driver's seat and takes off.

TOM:

I'm so sorry about this Anthony,
I really am.

ANTHONY BEANS:

Fuck you Tom!
Fuck all of you!

Billy knocks him out.
The mob takes off in a pick-up truck.
Back at the precinct,
everyone is watching the news.

TV NEWS:

As many of us can recall, 19 year-old Terrence Price was gunned down last year by three New York police officers. Martin Monroe, Jack Seiver, and Anthony Beans were all found not guilty of any wrong doing. We are closely reaching the hour point where Terrence Price's older brother, Kenneth Price has promised to destroy another precinct if he is not delivered at least one of these men.

REPORTER:

Excuse me sir, what do you think should be done?

CIVILIAN MAN:

I say throw them to this guy; it's about time cops started learning that their wrongful death shootings have consequences. LA had the 92 riots, New York has the 09 explosions.

TV REPORTER:

What about you ma'me do you feel the same way?

CIVILIAN WOMAN:

I say there has been enough bloodshed for one day, but if giving this man these two baby killers could put an end to all of this, then so be it.

CAPTAIN WILLIAMS:

I can't believe these people.

AGENT SNOW:

They say New York is the most hostile city. Now I believe it.

COMMISSIONER STYLES:

Hey, what you're seeing here is not my city, this is all your friend Price's doing!

MARTIN MONROE: (BARGING IN, SWEATING AND OUT OF BREATH)

You got that right.

CAPTAIN WILLIAMS:

Monroe?!

MARTIN MONROE:

Capt. You gotta help me, please, the whole city is looking for me.

CAPTAIN WILLIAMS:

Calm down son, you're safe now.

MARTIN MONROE: (LOOKING AT THE TV SET)

That's more than I could say about Beans.
They all look at the TV.

We're at the street where they have brought Anthony Beans.

BILLY:

What should we do?

TOM:

Just throw him out.

ANTHONY BEANS:

You guys are making a mistake,
you hear me, a mistake!

Kenneth Price's crew drives up on them.

KENNETH PRICE:

Hello gentlemen,
I see you've come bearing gifts.

TOM:

We don't know where Monroe is,
is this good enough?

KENNETH PRICE:

Yes, a precinct will be speared this hour.
You could leave now.

ANTHONY BEANS:

Tom don't you do this, don't you fucking do
this to me!

Tom and the rest of the mob take off,
leaving Anthony there for Price.

KENNETH PRICE:

Mr. Beans, how are you doing today?

ANTHONY BEANS: (SPITTING ON HIM)

Fuck you asshole, your brother was a clean shoot.

KENNETH PRICE: (WIPING THE SPIT OFF)

He didn't have a weapon on him, he was a good kid.
Now I would like for you to read this for me, please if you don't mind?

ANTHONY BEANS: (RIPPING THE PAPER UP)

I'm not reading anything; your nigger brother is dead, now deal with it.

KENNETH PRICE:

Men.

Price and two other foot soldiers pull out 9mm Berettas and execute him the same way they did Jack Seiver.

FOOT SOLDIER:

Two down Price.

KENNETH PRICE:

One to go.

Back at the Precinct.

MARTIN MONROE:

Jesus Christ Capt. Please don't let him kill me, not like that, please don't.

CAPTAIN WILLIAMS: (TAKING HIM TO THE BACK)

It's okay son, your safe here. Look I want you to stay back here okay. Don't leave this room, you understand me?

MARTIN MONROE:

Okay Capt. Thanks.
It looks different.

CAPTAIN WILLIAMS:

What?

MARTIN MONROE:

Seeing that. A cop on the receiving
end of three gunmen. It looks and feels
different.

**(Looking at the officer and seeing Terrence
Price's blooded and bullet filled body)**

I'm so sorry, I am so sorry.

CAPTAIN WILLIAMS: (TO THE OFFICER)

Listen to me, guard this room, no one goes
in or out.
You understand me officer, in or out.

OFFICER:

Yes sir.

As soon as the Captain walks off, that officer pulls out his
cell phone.

CAPTAIN WILLIAMS:

Look, we cannot do anything anymore,
we have to go in with what little we have.

AGENT SNOW:

That will be suicide!

CAPTAIN WILLIAMS:

We don't have a choice! Commissioner?

COMMISSIONER STYLES:

Do it, gather whatever man power you can
get, we'll head out before his next attack.

Agent gears walks off to the side,
Agent snow follows him.

AGENT SNOW:

Hey what's wrong with you?
You haven't spoken a word in over an hour.

AGENT GEARS:

I don't know what to think anymore,
about the job, Price, anything.

AGENT SNOW:

I need you to think clearly, you know what
type of weapons he has; they are going to b
slaughtered like lambs.

AGENT GEARS:

They, we don't have any other option to go
in after him. This has to be done.

COMMISSIONER STYLES:

Hey Gears are you in or out?

AGENT GEARS:

I'm in.
(He walks towards them)

Back at the warehouse.

FOOT SOLDIER:

Hey boss, our contact on the inside says
Monroe is there, and there's no way of us
getting him. They are planning a full on
assault led by your old partner.

FOOT SOLDIER 2:

They don't even know where we are?

KENNETH PRICE:

That won't stop them, they know were in the
general are, that's more than enough for
Gears.

FOOT SOLDIER 2:

So what do you want to do boss?

FOOT SOLDIER:

Price?!

KENNETH PRICE:

Give me your cell phone.

Back at the precinct,
Agent Gears picks up his cell phone.

AGENT GEARS:

Hello.

He looks at all of them with a shocking
look, they all look at him back.
Fade to Agent Gears bringing in Price
into the precinct, walking him into the
interrogation room. Price see's inside
contact, signaling where Monroe is being
protected.

Zoom in on both Price's and Gears face as they both have the
same flashback, where they are in an ATF's interrogation room.

KENNETH PRICE:

This is it, where all the magic happens
Joseph. We find out everything we need to
find out about our POI's.

AGENT GEARS:

Person Of Interest.

KENNETH PRICE:

That's right.

AGENT GEARS:

Any tips?

KENNETH PRICE:

Don't show emotion.
They both chuckle.

AGENT GEARS:

Right.

>   FADE BACK TO THEM ENTERING THE INTERROGA-
>   TION ROOM BACK AT THE PRECINCT. THE DOOR
>   CLOSES. CAPTAIN WILLIAMS TRIES TO GET IN;
>   BUT IS BLOCKED BE AGENT SNOW.

AGENT SNOW:

Where do you think you're going?

CAPTAIN WILLIAMS:

I have every right to be a part of this
interrogation.

AGENT SNOW:

You and I both know, once you go in there,
it won't be an interrogation. Now give me
the key.
Thank you, you could watch from the other
side like the commissioner, go on.

CAPTAIN WILLIAMS:

I'll have my moment, that's a promise.

They exchange unpleasant looks.

In the interrogation room, Price is sitting down looking
at his watch, Gears is standing up looking at him with
confusion.

AGENT GEARS:

Never in my wildest dreams, had I ever
thought for a second you and I would be on
opposite sides in this room.

KENNETH PRICE: (CHECKING HIS WATCH)

Hmmm.

AGENT GEARS:

I don't know why you keep looking at your
watch Price, you're not going anywhere.

KENNETH PRICE:

Is that so Joseph?

AGENT GEARS:

Yea Price that's so, you think your getting
off this or getting away with it?

KENNETH PRICE:

If history has taught us anything,
we badges get off with everything.

(Laughing follows)

AGENT GEARS: (SLAMMING THE TABLE)

You think this is funny Price, the body
count is massive.
Did you actually believe you could get away
with this?

KENNETH PRICE:

The lawyer for Monroe, Seiver, and Beans,
seems to be very proficient, maybe I get
him, if didn't die today that is.

AGENT GEARS:

No! No! Stop! Stop this right now,
this is not a game Price!

KENNETH PRICE:

You don't think I know this Joseph, after
the verdict came in, about my brother, I
knew we would be on opposite sides.

Agent Gears turns his head.

KENNETH PRICE: (SLAMMING THE TABLE AND RISING OF HIS CHAIR)

Don't you turn away from me Joseph!

Agent Gears backs up and reaches for his
gun. They stare at one another, knowing
what they have come down to.

Price seats back down.

KENNETH PRICE:

It was different.

AGENT GEARS:

What was?

KENNETH PRICE:

I didn't care about Rodney King, Amadou
Diallo, or even the Bell boy, none of them
made a difference to me. But my brother
was my brother; it was different when your
own families' blood is being spilled by the
badge, so different.

AGENT GEARS:

You have burned New York City, do you
understand that Price?

KENNETH PRICE:

I don't care, I told you,
I want……

AGENT GEARS:

I know what you want Price, blood for blood.
You've made that point perfectly clear, crystal clear. But the badge Kenneth, the oath we took as law enforcer's, you broke that, all of that.

KENNETH PRICE:

Don't you come at me with that Joseph, not me! I knew the job, I knew it well. But these pigs, these pigs go around gunning people down, innocent people; never once thinking what happens if they gunned down a family member that is related to a badge.

AGENT GEARS:

Innocent people. Innocent people Price. What the hell do you think you've been doing all day?! Why didn't you just take out this precinct? Huh? This is the precinct where those officers came from, why not take out this precinct and be done with it?

KENNETH PRICE:

Because.

AGENT GEARS:

Because what?

KENNETH PRICE:

Because when it is all said and done, when lives are restored to normal, there still going to need to place blame, and this precinct will be here.

AGENT GEARS:

They'll blame you Price.

KENNETH PRICE:

Not for why it all started, it will be this
precinct. They precinct that gave those
men, murderer's jobs, and the opportunity
to take the life of my brother. The city
will blame them.

(He checks his watch again)

Agent Gears walks out the room, and heads to the bathroom,
Agent Snow locks the room and follows him.

AGENT SNOW:

Are you okay?

AGENT GEARS:

I don't know who the hell is in there, but
that's not Price, you hear me that's not
Kenneth Price.

AGENT SNOW:

Look we need to get him out of here, get
him back to ATF headquarters, there's no
way in hell he's going to make it to trial,
they'll do to him what he has done to them.

AGENT GEARS:

Do unto others, as you would have others do
unto you.

AGENT SNOW:

Exactly.

AGENT GEARS:

So what do you suggest we do?

Simultaneously Commissioner Styles and
Captain Williams are conspiring right out
the interrogation room.

COMMISSIONER STYLES:

Look Williams, just unlock the door with
your extra key, and stand guard. Make sure
I'm not interrupted.

CAPTAIN WILLIAMS:

But sir, I think……

COMMISSIONER STYLES: (CUTTING HIM OFF)

Look Williams, I'll take care of this, I
promise, he'll pay.

CAPTAIN WILLIAMS: (UNLOCKING THE DOOR)

Yes Commissioner.

Commissioner Styles enters the room.

KENNETH PRICE:

Commissioner Styles, how are you?

COMMISSIONER STYLES:

Please, let's dispense with the
pleasantries'.

KENNETH PRICE:

Hmmm. Of course, what can I do for you?

COMMISSIONER STYLES:

Don't pretend you and I are buddy, buddy!

(He walks over to the same side of him)

My city is in turmoil because of you,
you have reduced it to rubble you sack of
shit.

Price just smiles.
OUTSIDE THE INTERROGATION ROOM.

AGENT SNOW:

What are you doing out here?
Where's the Commissioner?

CAPTAIN WILLIAMS:

Inside.

AGENT GEARS:

What?! Let us in.

CAPTAIN WILLIAMS:

Sorry, can't do.

Inside the interrogation room.

COMMISSIONER STYLES: (PULLING A GUN)

Any last words?

Price smirks and chuckles a little, he
kicks the knee caps of the commissioner,
you hear it snap, the commissioner screams
and fires a round into the floor and he drops
to his knees.

COMMISSIONER STYLES:

Ahhh! Son of a bitch!

The other's come barging inside.

CAPTAIN WILLIAMS:

Commissioner!

AGENT GEARS:

Price, don't do it!
Price grabs the commissioner's head and
snaps his neck.

He picks up the gun. Captain Williams and
Agent Gears have their weapons pointed at
Price.

CAPTAIN WILLIAMS:

Drop it you son of a bitch!

AGENT GEARS:

Price please, drop your weapon!
Price looks outside the door pass them, he
sees his man coming in about to assault the
precinct.

KENNETH PRICE:

If you haven't asked for God's help yet,
I can assure you, now would be the time.

Price flips the table that's in front of him
and gets down behind it. Captain Williams,
Agents Gears and Snow start to hear gun
shots and turn around. They return fire.
Agent snow is firing underneath the tables,
taking out the legs of the assailants,
Agents Gears is killing some of the foot
soldiers. Captain Williams is also hitting
his marks. Some of the officer's are being
taken out as well, both sides are receiving
casualties.

MARTIN MONROE: (FRANTIC)

Jesus Christ, they came for me, you gotta
get me out of here.

The officer just looks at him.

CAPTAIN WILLIAMS:

Hey gears, we gotta get Monroe out of here!

AGENT GEARS:

I'm more concerned about surviving this
first Williams!

Back in the interrogation room, Price sees he can't go out
that door, so he shoots three shots into the two-way mirror
wall, picks up a chair and tosses it to clear a way for

himself. He goes through, opens the door, checks to see if it is clear, gets out and heads for the room where Monroe is being protected.

He opens the door.

MARTIN MONROE:

Shoot him! What are you waiting for?!
Shoot him!

KENNETH PRICE:

Put handcuffs on him,
I don't want him to be too much trouble.

OFFICER:

Yes sir.

MARTIN MONROE: (FRANTIC)

Yes sir, are you shitten me?!
You are working for him?!
Monroe tries to fight them off, but they
both over power him with no problem. Price
grabs him and drags him outside the room.

As soon as Monroe is out, Agent Snow stops
them.

AGENT PRICE:

Freeze Price!

MARTIN MONROE:

Please help me!
Please I'm begging you!

AGENT SNOW:

Shut up! Price, please let him go,
it's over, you've lost.

KENNETH PRICE:

I can't do that Tanya, I've come this
far, I have waited this whole time to get
revenge for my brother, I will not turn
back now, I can't.

AGENT SNOW:

I can't let you walk out of here Price,
I won't do that.

The officer inside the room takes aim at
Agent Snow and shoots her three times in
the stomach, Agent Snow hand jerks and
squeezes the trigger, and a round goes off
into the shoulder of Martin Monroe.

MARTIN MONROE:

Ahhh! Fuck!

AGENT GEARS:

Tanya!!

He goes for her, still being shot at and returning fire.
Captain Williams is covering for him.

KENNETH PRICE:

Why did you do that?!

OFFICER:

Sorry sir,
I just thought……

KENNETH PRICE:

Forget it!
Let's go!

Those three take off. Get in a squad car
and drive off. Price is in the back with
Monroe, containing him, while the officer is
driving. It is pouring rain outside, and
the air is filled with debris.

AGENT GEARS:

Tanya, hold on baby, well get you some
help.

AGENT SNOW:

I'm sorry, so sorry.

AGENT GEARS:

Sorry? Sorry for what?
You didn't do anything wrong.

AGENT SNOW:

I couldn't pull the trigger; I thought I
could reach him, that our friend was still
in there somewhere. I love you Joseph,
I love you so much.

AGENT GEARS:

I love you too babe,
I love you too.

AGENT SNOW:

I would've said yes.

AGENT GEARS:

What?

AGENT SNOW:

If you'll proposed,
I would've said yes.

AGENT GEARS:

There's still time for all of that.

AGENT SNOW:

I love you Gears.

(She passes)

AGENT GEARS:

Nooo!!!!!!

Gears closes her eyes and pulls her in close to his chest. He places her head down gently and takes off after Price, Captain Williams sees Gears take off. Agent Gears gets into a squad car, the keys are in the glove box, he starts the car and take off. A car chase ensues. After an exhausting car chase, they get close to where Price was holding his executions. Before they could officially get there, a bus rams right into the driver, the car flips over, Agent Gears turns his car left, the car smashes into the side of the bus, but he doesn't suffer any severe injuries, but he is still banged up nonetheless. Price gets out of the totaled upside down car, he checks for the driver's pulse, the driver is dead. Price grabs Monroe and drags him out the car, they head towards the execution street. Agent Gears gets out, goes around the bus, he sees the dead officer, looks up and sees Price and Monroe running, he takes off after them.

KENNETH PRICE:

Get down.

MARTIN MONROE:

Please don't do this. What happened to
your brother was an accident. I swear it.

KENNETH PRICE:

A lot of accidents happen with you cops,
too much if you ask me. You should feel
so fortunate that I have resolved myself
to accept the fact that I have to kill you
with one gun instead of three. You won't
be executed like your friends, murdered
like my brother.

MARTIN MONROE:

Please I don't want to die!

KENNETH PRICE: (RISING THE GUN TO MONROE'S HEAD)

Neither did my brother Terrence.

(He pulls the trigger and shoots Monroe point blank in the head)

He lowers the gun to his side.

AGENT GEARS: (POINTING HIS GUN AT PRICE)

Drop it Price!

Price turns around to face Gears.

AGENT GEARS:

It's over Price, there all dead, You got your revenge!

KENNETH PRICE:

I'm not going in Joseph.

AGENT GEARS:

That is never their choice, not the other side, remember.

KENNETH PRICE:

Of course I remember,
I taught you that lesson.

AGENT GEARS:

It's over Price, over!

KENNETH PRICE:

I am not going in.

AGENT GEARS:

Please don't.

KENNETH PRICE:

I'm so sorry about Tanya, I loved you both so much, you were the only family I had left.

AGENT GEARS:

And I'm sorry about Terrence, Ken, he
didn't deserve that, no one does.

They stare at each other for a bit longer,
Price raises his arm, they both once again
just stare with widened eyes, you hear
four gun shots fire. Price drops to the
floor, Agent Gears looks behind him, and
sees Captain Williams. They stare at each
other, Agent Gears starts walking back,
heading towards Price. Price is coughing
up blood. Agent Gears gets down next to
him and supports his head.

AGENT GEARS:

Hey hold on, we'll get you some help.

KENNETH PRICE:

No please don't.I am sorry Joseph, I am.

AGENT GEARS:

I hope you find peace my friend.

Price is having one last flashback of him
and his brother.

They are in their mother's home kitchen
talking.

KENNETH PRICE:

So do you know what you want to do with
your life yet?

TERRENCE PRICE:

Yea I do.

KENNETH PRICE:

Oh, really, what's that?

TERRENCE PRICE:

An ATF special agent like my big brother.

KENNETH PRICE:

Oh is that so, why have you decided that career path?

TERRENCE PRICE:

Because you can't always be my keeper big brother, eventually I will have to learn to take care of myself, and what better to become an agent like my brother, anything you could do, I could do better.

They both laugh.

KENNETH PRICE:

I will always be your keeper, always.

They smile at one another.

FADE BACK.

KENNETH PRICE:

Bury me next to my brother, please Joseph.

AGENT GEARS:

Okay Price, okay. Kenneth Price passes.

Agent Gears closes his eyes.
Captain Williams walks up and stands over them.

FADE BACK AND OUT TO BLACK.

END CREDITS.

About the Author

The author brings a new perspective on the ideal of wrongful deaths by police officers. He is young and new to the writing game and is making his mark on the world one word at a time. While other writer's talk about reaching originality, this writer does so with great success and there is nothing he needs to be apologetic for.

Printed in the United States
by Baker & Taylor Publisher Services